Facing New Horizons Through
Active Children's Programs
LSCA Title I Grant
1987

Small Bear
Solves a Mystery

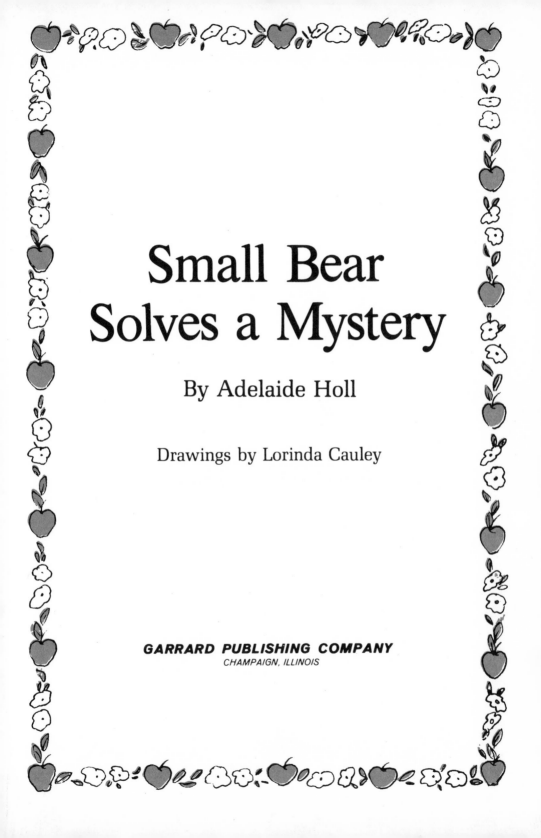

Small Bear
Solves a Mystery

By Adelaide Holl

Drawings by Lorinda Cauley

GARRARD PUBLISHING COMPANY
CHAMPAIGN, ILLINOIS

Library of Congress Cataloging in Publication Data

Holl, Adelaide.
  Small Bear solves a mystery.

  (Her Small Bear Adventures)
    SUMMARY: In search of an apple thief, Small
Bear and his friends find a hungry old bear whom
they decide to adopt.
    [1. Old age—Fiction. 2. Bears—Fiction]
I. Cauley, Lorinda. II. Title.
PZ7.H7078Sis   [E]   78-16727
ISBN 0-8116-4456-1

Small Bear Solves a Mystery

Small Bear sat by the door of his cave
and sniffed the good smells of summer.
There was the lovely smell of wet earth
after last night's rain.
There was the sweet smell of blossoms
on the berry bushes.

Sniff! Sniff!

Small Bear sniffed another smell.

It smelled like

something juicy and delicious.

"Apples!" thought Small Bear.

"Mother Bear is coming back

from the orchard

with sweet, ripe apples."

He jumped up

and ran to meet her.

"Mother Bear!"

he shouted excitedly.

"May I have some apples?

I want to have an apple party.

I want to invite Binky and April

to my apple party."

"That will be fine,"
said Mother Bear kindly.
"Here are a few of the apples.
The rest we must save for dinner."
Small Bear was delighted.

"I'll set a party table,"
he said excitedly.
He found leaves
to use as plates.
He picked flowers
to make the table pretty.

"The party will be fun," he thought.
When the table was all ready,
Small Bear looked it over.
Then he hurried down the forest path
toward the cave where Binky lived.
He found Binky and April
playing under a tall tree.
"Hi, Binky! Hi, April!"
called Small Bear.
"I'm having an apple party.
You are both invited."
Binky was delighted.
"That sounds like fun," he said.
"Yum, yum! Apples!"
said April, rubbing her tummy
with her little paw.

"Let's go!" shouted Small Bear.
And they all ran off together.
"Wait till you see my pretty table,"
Small Bear said proudly.
They ran down the forest path
until they came to the big stone
under the tall oak tree.

Then they stopped in surprise.
April looked mad.
"I don't think
your table is pretty,"
she said crossly.
"And I don't see any apples."

"Oh, dear me!"
cried Small Bear sadly.
"What a mess!
Somebody upset my flowers.
Somebody stole my apples."
Binky looked puzzled.
"But who would do that?"
he asked in surprise.
"Most of our forest friends
don't even *like* apples.
Beaver likes tree bark.
Turtle and frog and mole
eat mostly bugs."
Small Bear shook his head.
"Those are all my friends.
They wouldn't steal my apples."

April spoke up.
"I think somebody
is playing a trick on you.
Somebody hid the apples
just for fun."
Small Bear shook his head again.

"I don't think it's fun,"
he said to his friends.
Owl called down from his tree,
"What's all the fuss about?
All I hear down there
is chatter, chatter, chatter."

Small Bear looked up at Owl.

"Somebody stole my apples,"
he told Owl sadly.

"Well," said Owl wisely,
"why don't you become a detective?
Then you can try
to solve the mystery."

Small Bear looked puzzled.

"What's a detective?"
he asked.

"And what's a mystery?"

"A mystery is a kind of secret,"
said Owl.

"A detective is someone
who finds an answer
to the secret."

Small Bear thought for a minute.
"All right! I'll be a detective.
Binky and April can help me
solve the mystery.
What do we do first?"
Small Bear asked Owl.
"First, you look for footprints,"
Owl told the three little bears.

So Small Bear, Binky, and April
put their noses to the ground.
They started off, looking for footprints.
Owl put his head under his wing
and went back to sleep.
"Look here!" cried Small Bear.
"See these great big paw prints!"

"Let's follow them!" shouted Binky.
The little bears
began to follow the footprints.
They followed them
down a little path.
The footprints
went under a big bush.
The little bears stopped.

Carefully Small Bear looked
under the bush.
"Somebody has been here,"
he whispered to the others.
"Somebody was lying in the grass
under this bush.
And somebody was eating apples.
Look at all the apple cores."

Just then Robin peered out
from the leafy bush.
"What are you looking for,
Small Bear?"
she asked in a friendly voice.
"I'm looking for somebody
who took my apples,"
Small Bear told Robin.
"Did you see anybody
lying under this bush?"
"No," said Robin.
"I didn't see anybody.
But there *was* someone here.
Someone bumped against the bush.
He bumped so hard
I almost fell out of my nest."

April called excitedly,
"I see more footprints!"
Binky shouted,
"I see more apple cores!
Let's follow them!"

They followed a trail
of big paw prints.
They followed a trail
of apple cores.

The trail led them
down to the forest pond.
Then it stopped suddenly
beside a big fallen tree.

Small Bear said softly, "Shhhh!
Maybe the big somebody
is hiding behind that log."
The bears tiptoed up.
They peered over.

"Ohhhh!" they all cried
in surprise.
There behind the log
lay a big furry somebody.
The somebody was sound asleep.

Small Bear and Binky
looked a little scared.
But April didn't.
She gave the big somebody
a poke with a stick.

"Wake up!" she shouted.

The big somebody turned over.

"Ho, hum!" it growled.

Then the somebody sat up.

The somebody

was a great big brown bear.

Small Bear tried to look brave.

"Who are you?" he asked.

"What are you doing in our forest?

And why did you steal my apples?"

"I was hungry," said the big bear
in a deep, growly voice.
"I was very hungry."
"You spoiled my apple party,"
said Small Bear crossly.
The big bear looked sad.

"I'm sorry," he told Small Bear.
"I didn't know
those were your apples."
Small Bear asked again,
"Who are you?
And where did you come from?"

"I came down here
from the Great North Woods,"
said the big bear.
"It was getting too cold
for an old bear like me
to live up there.
Besides, it was hard
for me to find food.
I'm too old
to climb a bee tree
to look for honey.
And I'm not very good
at catching fish anymore."

Suddenly Small Bear felt sorry
for the big bear.
He held out his paw.

"My name is Small Bear,"
he said.
"This is my friend, Binky,
and this is his little sister, April.
Let's be friends."

"Let's *do* be friends,"
said the big bear.
Binky spoke up.
"Welcome to our forest."

April gave the big bear a hug.
"I think you're nice,"
she said.

"What is your name?"
Small Bear asked.
The big bear
gave Small Bear a pat.
"I would like you
to call me 'Grandfather,' "
he said.
April looked puzzled.
"What's a grandfather?"
she asked.
The big bear said kindly,
"A grandfather is someone
who holds you on his knee.
He is someone
who tells you stories.
He plays games with you."

"I'd like that," said April.

"So would I," said Binky.

"Me too," added Small Bear.

The big bear looked very happy.
Small Bear said to him,
"Please come home with me
and meet my mother.

I know she will want you
to stay for supper.
And you can sleep
in our cave tonight.
Tomorrow
we'll all help you
find a cave
of your own."
"And we'll take you to meet
all of our forest friends,"
added Binky.
April took
Grandfather Bear's paw.
"Tomorrow
will you tell me a story?"
she asked.

Grandfather Bear nodded.
Then they all set off happily
for Small Bear's home.